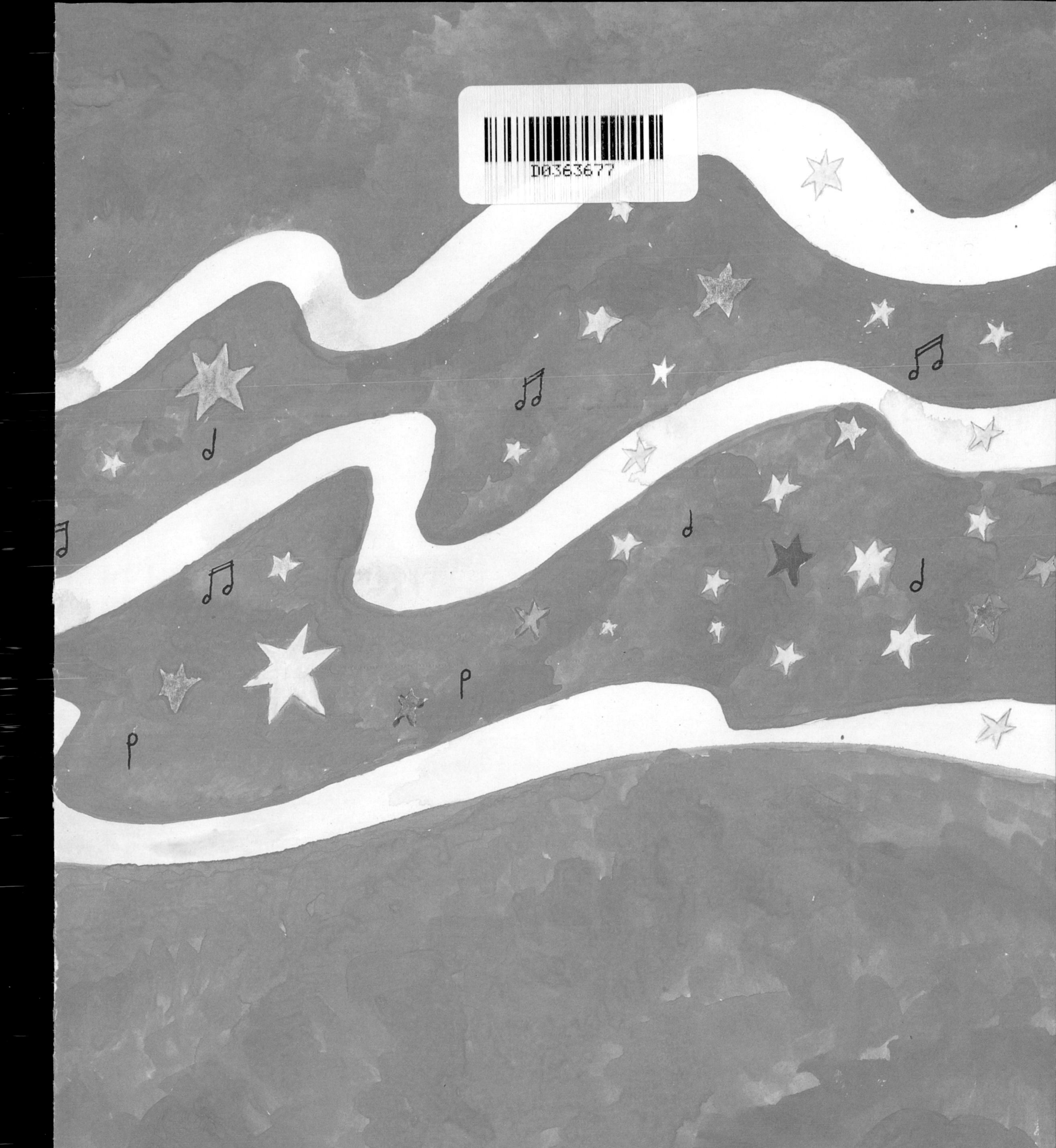

The Tale of GILBERT ALEXANDER PIG

Dedicated to
Gilbert Alexander Askey
who knows how to blow the biggest,
fattest 'G' you ever heard and knows
how to stand up and take his bow

Barefoot Books Ltd
PO Box 95
Kingswood
Bristol
BS30 5BH

This edition published in Great Britain in 2000 by Barefoot Books Ltd
Originally published in Australia in 1999 by Benchmark Publications Management Pty Ltd, Melbourne

This book is reproduced on 100% acid-free paper

Graphic design by Design/Section, Frome
Printed in Hong Kong/China by South China Printing Co. (1988) Ltd

ISBN 1 84148 214 5

British Cataloguing-in-Publication Data: a catalogue
record for this book is available from the British Library

1 3 5 7 9 8 6 4 2

The Tale of
GILBERT ALEXANDER PIG

written by
GAEL CRESP

illustrated by
DAVID COX

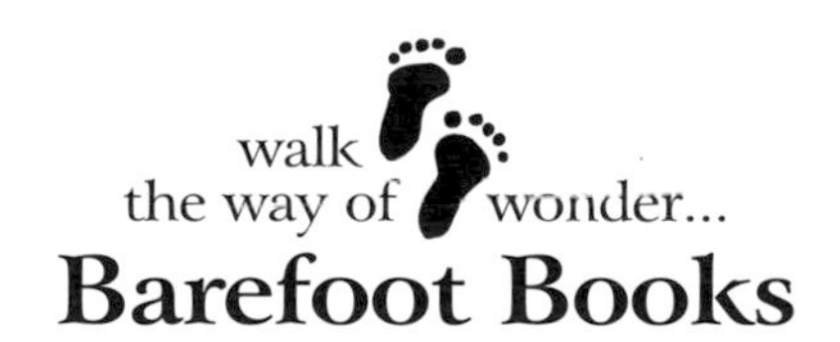

Once upon a time, there was a little black pig called Gilbert Alexander who decided it was time to make his way in the wide world. So he packed his knapsack, said goodbye to his mother, took his trumpet in his trotter and left home.

Gilbert Alexander Pig
walked and walked.

He walked all
morning and
all afternoon.

The sun was hot and
he was thirsty and tired,
and so when he came
to a river he sat
down to rest.

Gilbert Alexander Pig looked at the cool, clear water, the smooth speckled stones on the river bank and the tall, green trees. He said, 'I'm going to stay by this river. I'm going to catch myself a fish in the water, make myself a fire among the stones and cook that fish. And at night, I'm going to play my trumpet to the stars.'

And that's what he did.

When the nights got cold and the wind blew, Gilbert Alexander Pig took a piece of calico and some rope from his pack and rigged up a little shelter under the trees to keep out the draught. He caught some fish in the river and cooked them on the fire.

At night he played his trumpet to the stars. In fact, he played his trumpet all night and slept so long on the rocks by the river in the day that he only woke as the sun was setting.

Things went on very happily for some time, until, one night, the white Wolf heard the trumpet.

When he got close, the Wolf could smell the fire, and the fish, and eventually the little black pig. He crept closer and closer until finally he stuck his head around the calico shelter.

'Little pig, little pig, I'm going to knock down your shelter, I'm going to eat up your fish, I'm going to eat YOU up and I'm going to blow that trumpet MYSELF!'

'Oh no, not by the hair of my chinny chin chin. You are not going to take my TRUMPET!' shouted Gilbert Alexander Pig. He did not stay to argue. He just grabbed the trumpet and ran.

Now you might think that a wolf could run faster than a pig, and ordinarily you would be correct, but there was no way that Gilbert Alexander Pig was going to let the Wolf get his paws or his lips on that trumpet!

Early in the morning, Gilbert Alexander Pig stopped running and drew a deep breath. And another deep breath. He looked around and saw that he was on the top of a mountain and that the view was superb — he could see far into the distance in every direction.

'I'm going to stay on this mountain. I'm going to catch myself a fish in that stream down there, make myself a fire among the stones and cook that fish. And at night, I'm going to play my trumpet to the stars.'

And that's what he did.

When the nights got cold, Gilbert Alexander Pig used fallen twigs and branches to make himself a hut and at night he played his trumpet to the stars.

It was not long, however, before the Wolf heard the sound of the trumpet, smelt the smoke and the fish, and crept up on Gilbert Alexander Pig.

'Little pig, little pig, I'm going to knock down your hut,
I'm going to eat up your fish, I'm going to eat YOU up and
I'm going to blow that trumpet MYSELF!'

'Oh no, not by the hair of my chinny chin chin. You are not going to take my TRUMPET!' roared Gilbert Alexander Pig. He did not stay to argue. He just grabbed the trumpet and ran.

JAZZ NIGHTLY
TONIGHT

Gilbert Alexander Pig ran all night and all day until finally he reached the city, where he felt safe from the Wolf. He sat in the gutter and thought about what he should do next.

'I'm going to have to build myself a sturdy brick house with walls and a roof and windows and a door. I'll make a fireplace and a stove and I will lock that Wolf out. But first I'll have to earn some money.'

And that's what he did.

Gilbert Alexander Pig
took off his hat and put
it by his feet. He got out
his trumpet and began
to play.

He busked in the streets. He played in the cafés.

He performed in the nightclubs. He appeared in the concert halls.

And when he had enough money, Gilbert Alexander Pig put his trumpet safely down and set to work. He put a brick on a brick, and a brick on a brick, until he had made a perfectly lovely little house.

Every day, Gilbert Alexander Pig walked to the supermarket and bought a fish. He took it home and cooked it in a frying pan on the stove, and at night he sat by the window and played his trumpet to the stars.

But a fish from the supermarket does not taste
the same as one fresh from a stream.
A fish cooked in a frying pan on a
stove is nothing like one cooked
on the coals of an open fire.
And stars lose much of their
magic when viewed through
a glass window.

Gilbert Alexander Pig was glad in the end when
the Wolf turned up.

'Little pig, little pig, I'm going to knock down your house, I'm going to eat up your fish, I'm going to eat YOU up and I'm going to blow that trumpet MYSELF!'

'Oh no, not by the hair of my chinny chin chin. There is no way you are going to take my trumpet!' sighed Gilbert Alexander Pig.

'We need to talk about this,' he said. 'I'll listen to you. You listen to me. And after we've talked it through, we will work out what we both want. We'll find a way that makes us BOTH happy!'

And so Gilbert Alexander Pig and the Wolf talked and talked. They talked all day and all night. Then they started to write. At last, they made an agreement, which they both signed.

In the summer, Gilbert Alexander Pig and the Wolf lived down by the river. The Wolf caught some fish and cooked them over the coals of the open fire and, at night, Gilbert Alexander Pig played his trumpet to the stars.

In the autumn, Gilbert Alexander Pig and the Wolf lived up on the mountain. The Wolf caught some fish and cooked them over the coals of the open fire.

And at night, Gilbert Alexander Pig played his trumpet to the stars.

But when the weather got really cold, Gilbert Alexander Pig and the Wolf lived in the little brick house in the city.

Every day, Gilbert Alexander Pig walked to the supermarket and bought two fish.

He took them home and cooked them in a frying pan on the stove, and at night he taught the Wolf how to play the trumpet.

And they lived happily ever after.

walk
the way of wonder...

Barefoot Books

The barefoot child represents the person who is in harmony with the natural world and moves freely across boundaries of many kinds. Barefoot Books explores this image with a range of high-quality picture books for children of all ages. We work with artists, writers and storytellers from many cultures, focusing on themes that support independence of spirit, encourage openness to others, and foster a life-long love of learning.

www.barefoot-books.com